THE JERSEY

FIGHT FOR YOUR RIGHT

THE JERSEY

FIGHT FOR YOUR RIGHT

Adapted by Paul Mantell
Based on the series created by Gordon Korman

New York

Printed in the United States of America

First Edition
1 3 5 7 9 10 8 6 4 2

Library of Congress Catalog Card Number: 00-109808

ISBN 0-7868-4466-3
For more Disney Press fun, visit www.disneybooks.com

CONTENTS

THE JERSEY

FIGHT FOR YOUR RIGHT

CHAPTER ONE

GOING . . . GOING . . . GOT!

Nick Lighter stepped up to the plate. He gripped the bat tightly and went into his stance, staring out at the mound. It was a beautiful Sunday afternoon in Fairfield. Nick breathed in the fresh, clear air and smiled. It was the perfect day for the Monday Night Football Club to dust off their mitts and get some practice at the Fairfield High baseball field.

But Nick wasn't thinking about the

beautiful weather. He was totally focused on only one thing—hitting a home run. He squinted hard, trying to intimidate the pitcher. Not that the pitcher was likely to be intimidated. After all, he was Nick's good friend Elliott Rifkin. But that was how they played—all of them in the Monday Night Football Club—totally seriously. As if they were in the big game.

"Rifkin, into the windup . . ." Elliott narrated as he swung his arms back and forth, back and forth.

"Sometime today would be nice," Coleman "'Slaw" Galloway said from behind the plate. "All this crouching is giving me leg cramps."

Elliott scowled at the catcher, then proceeded to shake off the first four signs 'Slaw gave him.

'Slaw groaned. "Come on, man!" he

complained. "I've only got five fingers!"

Nick saw his cousin Morgan out in center field, pounding her glove as if she was getting tired of waiting for Elliott to get on with it. She's probably trying to keep herself awake, Nick thought.

Morgan was playing him way too shallow, Nick noticed with annoyance. Didn't she have any respect for his power with the bat? Nick waved the bat over his shoulder, impatient for the pitch.

"Let's go, Elliott!" he shouted. "While we're *young*!"

Elliott finally finished his windup. He spun and fired, and the ball came rocketing toward home plate.

Perfect, Nick thought. It was a big, fat batting-practice fastball, right over the heart of the plate. Nick swung so hard he nearly flew out of his shoes.

THE JERSEY

CRACK! The ball made contact with the bat right on the sweet spot, and went sky high.

Morgan got a late jump on the ball. As Nick jogged slowly toward first base, doing his home-run trot, a sly grin came over his face. "Whoo-oo!" he yelled. "Nick Lighter . . . goin' for the fences, baby! That ball's outta here!" As long as he'd hit a home run, he figured he might as well crow about it a little . . . or a lot.

Morgan was running like the wind now, trying to catch up to Nick's rocket shot. There's no way, he thought happily. Let her wear herself out—she'll never catch it. "That ball's outta here!" he shouted again, hoping she could hear him.

Morgan and Nick were good friends as well as cousins. But ever since she'd moved to Fairfield and become part of the Monday Night Football Club (MNFC for short), they'd also been rivals. They were both good athletes and fiercely competitive. Nick couldn't stand it when Morgan beat him at something, which she did more than half the time.

Not this time, though, Nick thought as he rounded first base. "That ball's outta he—"

He choked on the last word. Morgan ran straight up the wall, leaped into the air, stretched out her glove—and came down with Nick's monster shot! Nick's whole body deflated like a popped balloon.

"Youuuuu're out!!!" 'Slaw yelled in his umpire voice, punching the air enthusiastically. "What a catch, Morgan! Awesome!"

Morgan trotted toward home plate for her turn at bat. She waved the ball at

Nick, smiling, as if she thought he'd be happy for her. Yeah, right.

"I believe sandlot baseball history has been made," Elliott said seriously.

Nick glared at him. "It wasn't *that* great a catch!" he insisted.

Morgan stopped in her tracks and raised her eyebrows, surprised. Nick just turned his back on her and headed for the bench, boiling with fury. She'd done it to him again! Why did she always have to try to outdo him? He hated, hated, hated it!

I'm sorry that I ever let Morgan wear the magic jersey, Nick thought. After all, it's not like I *have* to share it. Our grandpa left the jersey to me—not her. I could have kept it all to myself—that would have outdone her . . . big time! The jersey was the most amazing thing that had ever happened to Nick—somehow, it had the mysterious power to transport anyone who wore it into the body of a real-life sports star! Of course, the jersey's power was a huge secret. No one knew what it could do, except for the members of the MNFC.

Nick had let 'Slaw and Elliott use the jersey. He'd let Morgan use it too, of course. And even though Nick sometimes thought he should have kept the jersey all to himself, he knew that he didn't really have a choice about sharing it. The jersey seemed to have a way of selecting who would wear it next. . . .

Wearing the jersey had changed them all. They'd each experienced sports at the highest level, and none of them would ever forget it. It made them closer to each other—and also more competitive.

Maybe *too* competitive, in Morgan's

case, Nick thought. Deep down, he knew that he was being unfair, but he was too angry to care. Right now, Nick wished Morgan had never seen the jersey.

And all he could think about was how he wouldn't let her beat him out again.

The four members of the MNFC walked down the main hall of Fairfield High School together the next morning. It was Monday, but it wasn't football season. That meant that they were temporarily the Monday Night *Baseball* Club, and they'd catch the big Yankees game together in Nick's den tonight. Morgan couldn't wait. She loved to watch Derek Jeter work his magic at shortstop.

"I still can't get over that catch from yesterday," 'Slaw said, shaking his head and smiling at the memory. "Morgan was playing the wall like Rickey Henderson! Ha ha!"

"It was amazing," Elliott agreed. Turning to Morgan, he asked, "How do you jump so high?"

"Look," Morgan said, enjoying the moment, "you don't think I took ballet lessons just for the tutus, do you?"

"You took ballet?" 'Slaw asked, his eyes wide. "*You*?" he repeated.

"Three years of it." Morgan shrugged. "A lot of athletes use it to train," she added.

"Oh, spare me." Nick rolled his eyes. "C'mon, guys," he said to 'Slaw and Elliott. "Let's '*train*'!" He pranced around on his tippy-toes, hands high over his head. Coleman and Elliott mimicked him, turning around and around in the middle of the hallway.

Morgan cocked an eyebrow. "Is that *Swan Lake*?" she asked. "Or *Swan Lame*?"

"Shh! Quiet!" Nick insisted. "We're in serious training!"

"Oh, you're so hilarious. . . ." Morgan was starting to get annoyed.

Nick, 'Slaw, and Elliott's little show had attracted a small crowd. Among them, Morgan spotted two really cute girls— Amanda Snowden and Tami Harper. She knew Nick had a crush on Amanda, and that Elliott and 'Slaw talked all the time about how pretty Tami was.

"Yes, you're very funny," Morgan said, a sly smile playing on her face. "Funny *looking*, that is," she added, waving to Amanda and Tami. "Hi, Amanda! Hi, Tami!" she shouted.

The boys turned around, horror written all over their faces. Immediately, they began smoothing down their hair and clearing their throats in a desperate attempt to look cool. Too late. Amanda and Tami were falling all over themselves laughing and pointing at them.

Nick and Elliott were beet red, Morgan noted with satisfaction. 'Slaw had his face in his hands, as though he were trying to hide.

"Okay," Nick said, in a tough-as-nails voice, trying to cover his embarrassment. "Training's over. Let's get ready for try-outs."

Morgan snapped to attention. "Try-outs? You mean baseball tryouts?" she asked excitedly, forgetting everything else.

"Yeah," Coleman said. "Hey, aren't girls' softball tryouts today, too?"

Morgan knew he was probably just

trying to be helpful, but she bristled at 'Slaw's suggestion. "No way!" she said hotly. "I play baseball, not softball! I'm the best shortstop here!"

Nick tried to stifle a laugh. "Uh, sorry," he said, shaking his head. He made a buzzing sound, as if Morgan had answered wrong on a game show. "That would be me."

"No way, Morgan!" 'Slaw protested. "You can't try out for the high school baseball team!" He laughed as though it was the dumbest idea he'd ever heard.

That really got Morgan steamed. Hadn't they been playing ball with her just yesterday? Had they already forgotten what a great fielder she was? "You guys missed out on nineteen hits, thanks to me," she reminded them.

Elliott cast a doubtful glance at 'Slaw

and Nick. "Ah, yes," he said, nodding sagely. "The very difficult-to-verify stats of the sandlot league."

What?! Morgan couldn't believe it! Was Elliott trying to deny what they'd all seen with their own eyes? He had some nerve! They *all* did!

"Morgan," Nick said, patting her gently on the shoulder, "this is the real deal. Hardball. Overhand pitch? Come on," he added, as if she were being ridiculous. "I mean, us guys'll be lucky to get on the team ourselves—we're only freshmen. But you? Morgan, be reasonable. No girl's ever been on that team."

"I don't think any *normal* kid's ever been on the team," Elliott added. "The coach is 'old-school,'" he explained to Morgan, who after all, was pretty new in town. "Animals only."

"Grrrr," 'Slaw growled, pressing home the point.

Morgan folded her arms across her chest and set her jaw stubbornly. "This is America," she told the boys. "If I'm good enough, I'll make the team. And if I make the team, the coach has to play me." She turned on her heel and stalked away, heading for her first class of the day.

Behind her, she heard 'Slaw say, "She's got a point."

Well, of course I do, Morgan thought. And if 'Slaw could see it, surely the coach would, too. After all, Coach Bender was a teacher—an adult. Surely he'd be more mature than a bunch of freshman boys!

CHAPTER TWO

STRIKE ONE, YOU'RE OUT!

After school, Morgan hustled to her locker. She stowed her bookbag, took out her mitt, and headed for the athletic fields behind the school. She passed the infield where a few girls were already tossing the ball around, warming up for softball team tryouts.

Morgan frowned. Part of her actually wanted to join the softball team. It would be a great way to make new friends. Of course Morgan loved the Monday Night Football Club, but sometimes she got sick of hanging out with boys only.

But my game is baseball, Morgan thought, not softball. Besides, the fact that the guys had told her that she couldn't possibly make the all-boys' team only made her more determined to prove them wrong.

She strode right past the softball diamond, heading for the new ball field, where tryouts for the Fairfield Eagles— the school's renowned baseball team— were about to take place.

There had to be fifty kids mobbing the field, tossing balls around, throwing each other grounders and pop-ups . . . and every single one of them was male. Morgan swallowed hard, and made for the dugout.

STRIKE ONE, YOU'RE OUT!

Morgan looked at the ground as she walked, but she could feel the boys staring at her. Whatever—she wasn't going to let their stares get to her. She was here to try out, just like they were, and Morgan was sure she had as much talent as the best of the freshmen, which had to mean she had a decent chance of making the team.

Morgan looked around. She saw Nick standing in center field, tossing a ball back and forth with 'Slaw and Elliott. She took her mitt out of her gym bag and headed out to join them.

"Come on, Nick," Morgan heard 'Slaw shout as she approached. "Your arm is sorry! Throw it a little harder!"

Morgan stifled a giggle. Nick really was soft-tossing it up there. Maybe he was saving his arm strength for the tryout.

Good idea, she noted, deciding to do the same. Instead of throwing the ball to someone, she got down on the ground and went into her ballet stretches—which of course, also worked perfectly well for baseball.

She caught some of the guys watching her, smiling and shaking their heads. Is it because of the ballet stretches? she wondered. Or was it just because she was a girl, trying out for a "guys'" team? Well, she'd show them. It took strength and flexibility, not to mention grace and athletic ability, to do ballet. If she could dance on *pointe* she could certainly keep up with any of them.

She got up, looking around for the coach. He was standing by home plate, scribbling notes on a clipboard. Coach Bender was tall, balding, and muscular. A silver whistle hung around his neck. He looked to Morgan like a no-nonsense kind of guy. Well, that was fine with her. She was all business herself, when it came to making the team.

Nick tapped Morgan on the shoulder. "You're really doing this?" he asked, looking concerned. What's he so worried about? she wondered. That I'll get my feelings hurt? Or is it that I might actually make the team . . . and he might not?

"I am absolutely doing this," Morgan replied. She looked Nick in the eye with a don't-try-to-stop-me gaze.

Elliott had joined them, but he was staring toward home plate. "Uh-oh," he said softly. "Disturbance in the force." He put his hands over his ears just as Coach Bender blew his whistle.

Morgan covered her ears and winced.

Why are coaches' whistles always so loud? she wondered. Is there an athletic advantage in breaking the sound barrier, or something?

Coach Bender slowly surveyed the mass of boys who had come down to try out. Then his eyes fell on Morgan. He chuckled and shook his head. "Every year, there's always one," he said.

Morgan swallowed hard. "Uh-oh," she said under her breath as he walked right up to her.

"All right, listen up, grunts," Coach Bender said to the assembled crowd of hopefuls. "And grunt-ette," he added, jerking his head in Morgan's direction.

Oh, no! Morgan thought, horrified. He's a total caveman!

"The Fairfield Eagles are a championship team," the coach continued, turning slowly so he could make eye contact with each of them. "That's because I'm the best coach in the state," he said proudly. Morgan had to stifle a snort. "And if I keep turning out championship teams, then I can get a real job," he went on, "like at a State College. . . ."

"Well," Elliott muttered softly, "he sure doesn't lack confidence."

The coach snapped out of his reverie, and wheeled around in their direction. "No talking!" he barked. Obviously, he had eyes in the back of his head, not to mention supersensitive hearing.

How can he stand the whistle? Morgan wondered.

"Now," the coach continued, "as I look out over your young and hopeful faces, I can see that most of you are doomed to fail—so let's just get the inevitable over with. Hustle up to the position you want to play. Let's go! Hustle up! Uh, wait," he said, turning to a couple of the less athletic-looking kids. "Not you, you, you, and you. You guys hit the bench."

"A caveman!" Morgan repeated to herself, stunned. She wondered for a second whether she'd even want to play for someone as mean as Coach Bender. She sighed. It would be worth it to be on a team like the Eagles, she decided. She trotted out to the shortstop hole, shaking her head.

Elliott was jogging toward the pitcher's mound when he heard the coach's voice behind him. "Hey, you!"

Elliott swung around, pointing to himself. "Me?"

"Yeah, you. Chatter-boy." The coach smirked. "Batter up."

Elliott grinned. Coach wants me to bat first, he thought happily. This guy sure can spot talent! "The name's Rifkin, sir. Elliott Rifkin."

The coach didn't crack a smile. "I don't care if it's Sammy Sosa," he said, planting his hands on his hips. "Batter *up!*"

Elliott hustled to the plate, slightly deflated. Oh, well, he decided, coaches are always extra-hard on the really good players. Elliott grabbed a helmet and put it on. It was way too big. It came down over his eyes. He took it off and tried another. Still too big!

"I said batter up!" the coach yelled.

"Coming!" Elliott said, trying to sound cheerful and cooperative. He grabbed what looked like the smallest helmet and put it on. Even this one was too big for him, but at least he could see—kind of.

Then he took the shortest, lightest bat on the rack and stepped up to the plate.

The pitcher facing him was Rocco Baldessari, the Eagles' star right-hander. Rocco was a junior. He had to be at least six feet tall. Elliott was exactly five feet.

I guess I won't bother trying to intimidate him with the patented MNFC steely-eyed stare, Elliott thought. He scooted well back from the plate. It might be harder to reach the ball from where he was, but there was also less chance of him getting hit by Rocco's seventy-five-mile-per-hour fastball!

Morgan had gone out to play shortstop—*her* position. She figured not too many kids would be trying out for shortstop. It was the toughest position to field, except maybe for catcher. Sure enough, there were only three other kids standing there with her . . . and one of them was Nick!

He *would* do a thing like that, Morgan thought angrily, taking a place right in front of him.

Nick saw her and frowned.

Morgan lifted her eyebrows. *"What?"* she challenged him.

"You know shortstop is my position," Nick said, like he owned it or something.

"So?" Morgan asked, standing her ground. "It's mine, too."

"Whatever," Nick said disgustedly. "Just get ready to back me up." He moved a few steps forward, so that he was in front of her.

Morgan fumed. "You'll be the one riding the bench, not me," she muttered. She stood behind him, content to wait her turn. She'd show him . . . just like she'd shown him yesterday!

"Stee-rike one!" Coach Bender bellowed.

Elliott hadn't even seen the ball. There had been a blur coming out of Rocco's hand, then a buzzing sound as the ball zipped by him, landing in the catcher's mitt with a loud pop. Elliott shook his head rapidly to get the cobwebs out. Had Rocco really thrown a pitch? How could anybody throw that fast?

Elliott felt himself starting to panic. He gripped the bat tighter—so tightly that his palms grew sweaty and the bat became even harder to hold. Rocco wound up and fired again. Elliott closed his eyes and swung.

"Stee-rike two!" Coach Bender shouted gleefully. Then he turned toward the pitcher, who was already rubbing up the ball for the next pitch. "Hey, Rocco," he said, "why don't you go ahead and, uh, gift-wrap one for him, huh?"

Elliott could feel his cheeks burning. He held the bat high, ready to swing with all his might. He would show the coach he was no scrub. Gift-wrap, huh? Well, Elliott was not one to turn down a gift. This pitch was *his*.

Rocco wound up and fired. From the motion of his body, it looked like it was going to be another fastball. Elliott started his swing. Too late, he realized that Rocco had fooled him, throwing him an extra-slow change-up!

Elliott swung hard—so hard that his too-large helmet fell down over his eyes. Still, even though he couldn't see anything, he felt the bat make contact with the ball.

"Attaboy!" Coach Bender yelled. "It's a home run!"

Elliott dropped his bat and adjusted his helmet so he could see. He looked up, but none of the outfielders seemed to be moving to get his ball. "A home run! Really?" he gasped excitedly.

"No," the coach said, as the pathetic little squib fly landed right at Elliott's feet. "I'm sorry," the coach corrected himself. "I meant *run home*. Strike three, Rifkin. You're outta here." The coach yanked his thumb upward to signal that Elliott's turn at bat—and tryout—were both over.

Elliott was stunned. Flabbergasted. "But—but I was just warming up!" he protested meekly.

"Hit the dugout," the coach told him, in no uncertain terms. "Do your squawkin' walkin', son." Not wasting another moment on Elliott, he turned to the other kids, who were looking on in sober silence. "Okay, who's next?" he challenged. Nobody stepped forward.

Elliott kicked the dust in disgust. Who did that coach think he was, anyway? Elliott knew it would be idiotic to try to argue with him. He knew he ought to keep his mouth shut, and take this injustice like a man. He *knew* it—but he just couldn't make himself *do* it.

"You can't cut somebody after one at-bat!" Elliott blurted. "That's some kind of . . . discrimination!"

"Blah, blah, blah," the coach mocked him, smiling a crooked smile. "Tell it to yoout, simmerin

Th way, then took up a bat and a ball. "Hey, girlie!" he called out to Morgan. "All right, it's your turn. Look alive!"

Elliott turned and watched as the coach hit a sharp grounder to Morgan. She fielded it cleanly, and tossed a strike to first base.

Great, Elliott thought. She's gonna make the team, and I'm not. How totally humiliating!

Sitting in the dugout with him were the other kids who had already been cut. Elliott squirmed uncomfortably. These kids weren't athletes—not like *he* was! Okay, so baseball wasn't his best sport, but he didn't belong with these scrubs! Most of them were even shorter than he was!

"Why me?" he asked out loud. "Always me! Protein shakes, vitamins. And for what? It's a conspiracy against the little guy, I tell you!"

Elliott felt a sudden knot of tension

forming in his stomach. "Hey," he asked the kid sitting next to him, "how do you know if you're getting an ulcer?"

The kid just stared back at him, which only made Elliott more furious. *My baseball career is over before it's even begun, and this kid is looking at me like I'm crazy!* Elliott figured he'd better do something to release his frustration.

Elliot spied a bucket of baseballs on the ground next to him and gave it a vicious kick. The bucket spilled over, and the balls rolled out, bumping a stack of bats nearby. The bats began to topple over like a bunch of dominoes. Finally, the last bat went over. It hit the lever of an idle baseball pitching cannon.

Suddenly, the cannon went into action. It wound up and fired a curveball right through the dugout and onto the field, where it hit Coach Bender with a thud. Right between the eyes!

The coach dropped to the ground. A huge gasp of horror went up from all the assembled kids.

"Uh-oh," said Elliott.

Now he'd done it.

CHAPTER THREE

REBEL WITH A CAUSE

As school ended the following day, Elliott pulled open the door of room 203—Coach Bender's Health Education classroom. Inside, the coach was writing something on the blackboard. Elliott stepped inside so he could see it: WELCOME TO DETENTION, it read.

Elliott walked up to the coach. "I'm really sorry, Coach Bender," he said sincerely, with an extra dash of niceness thrown in.

Hearing his voice, the coach stiffened and turned to face his accidental attacker. He was wearing a big bandage across the bridge of his nose. "Oh, the pain," Coach Bender said in a toneless voice. "It suddenly subsided. Thank you, Rifkin." He glowered at Elliott.

Elliott hesitated for a moment, not sure if he should say something else. Finally, he decided it could only do more harm than good. Sighing, he took a seat in the far corner of the room.

The PA crackled. "Coach Bender," a voice squawked over the system, "To the main office. Coach Bender to the main office."

The coach stood up and pointed at Elliott. "Don't you try anything while I'm gone," he warned.

Elliott gulped, then heaved a sigh of relief as the coach left the room.

Once the door was safely closed, Elliott dared to glance around to see who else was suffering detention today. Ah, yes, he thought, the usual suspects. Rory Bunkley and all his tough-guy friends were there. It figured. They got detention practically every week. Elliott usually steered way clear of them. They were bad news, and everybody knew it.

They looked at him now as if he had dropped into the room straight from Mars. Then Rory got up and slowly came over to sit next to Elliott. "You?" he whispered. "It's *you*?"

"Uh . . ." Elliott whispered warily. "Are you gonna hurt me?"

"Me? Nah." Rory leaned in toward Elliott, a gleam in his eye. "I heard you knocked Bender out cold," he said under his breath.

"No . . . A bump is all . . . Really—it was

just an accident!" Elliott insisted.

"Yeah, sure," Rory said with a disbelieving smile. "Like I 'accidentally' tipped over the principal's car." He guffawed, and gave Elliott a friendly poke with his elbow. "You know," he said, "I always thought that you were a squid. . . ." He put his arm around Elliott's neck. "But maybe you got some potential."

Elliott's eyes widened, and a surprised smile came over his face. "Me?" he gasped. "I have potential?" Potential as a tough guy? Elliott could hardly imagine it.

Elliott thought of Coach Bender, and how the muscle-bound teacher had pushed him around. Suddenly, he could see himself in a whole new way—Elliott the bad boy . . . Elliott the rebel. Hmmm . . . he kind of liked the idea, actually.

Yes, it had a lot of appeal. . . .

The list of students who had made it through the first round of baseball try-outs was posted on the athletic department's bulletin board, in the hall outside the gym. A group of kids stood around it, looking for their names. From the disappointed looks on their faces, Nick guessed they hadn't found them.

The group of kids slunk away as Nick, Coleman, and Morgan stepped up to examine the list. "Yes!" Nick cried as he saw his own name halfway down the page. Okay, it was misspelled, but he could forgive Coach Bender for his ignorance. "Nick Liter, shortstop," would do just fine, thank you.

"Hel-lo!" 'Slaw said happily as he found his name under "catcher."

"All right!" Morgan cried, giving 'Slaw

a high five. Her name was on the shortstop list, too. In fact, she and Nick were two out of only three names under the position.

But Nick wasn't about to let Morgan get too excited. "You still have a long way to go before you make the team," he reminded her.

Morgan's smile faded, and her eyes narrowed as she looked back at him. "So do *you*," she shot back.

"All right, you juvenile delinquents," Coach Bender announced after only an hour of tortured silence, "this is your lucky day. I'm letting you all out of here early, on account of I've got baseball tryouts to take care of. But don't get any ideas. Any of you gets into any trouble today, you're gonna be spending a whole lotta time in here. Understand?"

Grunts of agreement were heard from all the assembled prisoners. The coach opened the door, and the detainees filed out, looking at the floor. Elliott was the last to leave. "Rifkin," Coach Bender stopped him at the door.

"Yes, Coach?"

"That goes double for you."

"Huh?"

"I hear the faintest whisper about you getting into trouble, you'll get double the detention of anybody else. Get it?"

Elliott swallowed hard. "Uh-huh," he said meekly.

"Good. Now get out of here."

Elliott did. He headed straight for his locker. He intended to get home before he accidentally did something that might keep him in detention *forever*.

But he was too late. Rory Bunkley was

waiting for him. The "Line of Pain"—that was what Rory's friends liked to call themselves—stood behind him, staring at Elliott with grim faces.

"Hey, squid!" Rory greeted him. "Oh, wait, you're not a squid. You got an upgrade—what's up, E-dog?"

Elliott blinked, surprised. "'E-dog?'" he said slowly. "I like that!" A grin spread across his face. Yeah . . . he was no longer just plain Elliott Rifkin, too short to be respected. He was the notorious E-dog, scourge of Fairfield High. No longer would Neanderthals like Coach Bender intimidate him. He was E-dog, and he had a crew to back him up.

Seeing the other kids staring at him, he practiced his "tough" look, snarling at them. "So," he said to Rory. "What are you guys up to?"

"Oh . . . just looking for trouble," said Rory, an evil grin appearing on his pimply face.

"Well, you found him," Elliott said, cracking his knuckles and slicking his hair back. "I feel *dangerous*."

CHAPTER FOUR

CUT TO THE BONE

It was a hot, humid afternoon, and the air was thick with dust from the infield. There were fewer than half as many kids this time as last, Morgan noticed hopefully. Then she saw Nick, who was occupying his usual position—otherwise known as *Morgan's* usual position: shortstop.

The kid on first base was throwing infield grounders to the other early arrivals. Nick fielded his chance cleanly, and tossed a strike to first. Then he turned and waved at Morgan, as if to say, "did you see that?"

Yes, she'd seen it. Yes, she knew he was a good fielder. She also knew she was better. And if this was any kind of fair try-out, she was going to prove it.

Morgan caught movement out of the corner of her eye. She spun around, and threw up her glove hand defensively— just in time to snag the ball the first base-man had thrown at her. "Hey!" she yelled at him. "What are you doing?"

"Sorry!" the kid called out to her. "I thought you were playing third."

I'm standing in foul territory, for Pete's sake, Morgan thought with annoyance. The first baseman snickered, and she realized he'd been trying to catch her off-guard.

Morgan sighed heavily. Some boys could be so stupid.

"You're back?" Coach Bender said to Morgan as he walked onto the infield.

She played it cool. "You put my name on the list," she replied. "I don't scare off that easily, Coach," she added, just to show him how gritty and gutsy she was.

"Well," the coach responded, unimpressed, "yesterday was 'warm-ups.' Today, we 'practice.'" Turning away from her, he blew his whistle. "All right, everybody. Let's go. Let's go. Hustle up. Hustle up. Let's go. Let's go."

What a jerk, Morgan said to herself. Why do I even want to play on his team?

Because, she answered herself, you love baseball. That's why.

The athletes moved quickly across the field. "Hudson! Heads up!" called the kid at first base. He threw his best fastball at her. She snagged it—then winced in pain.

"Owww!" she cried, taking off the glove and shaking her hand out.

"Tough it up, Hudson," the coach said with a snort.

Morgan held her tongue. She felt like telling him she was being picked on; that it wasn't fair, but she knew he wouldn't listen. Coach Bender was just like that kid on first base. They were both trying to keep her down! Well, she wouldn't let them beat her. She'd tough it up, just like the coach said!

Practice quickly went from bad to worse. Although Morgan made several snappy plays in the field, she threw the ball away twice. Maybe it was because she was trying to throw too hard, just to show that kid at first base that two could play at his game.

For the rest of the afternoon, the coach said nothing when she did well, but sure enough, he made a wisecrack whenever she messed up. When the kid at second tripped her on purpose as she tried to stretch the double she'd just hit into a triple, she got to third late, and Nick tagged her out.

"Hudson," yelled the coach, "you can't get to third by crawling!"

Everyone laughed at her. Morgan dusted herself off and saluted. "Got it, Coach!" she said enthusiastically.

When the coach turned his back, Nick came up to Morgan. "Rough day?" he asked.

Morgan scowled at him. "It seems to be rougher for me than for any of you guys. But, I love baseball, so it's what I have to do."

CUT TO THE BONE

At that moment, they heard Coach Bender yelling at a chubby kid who was running the bases, chugging and puffing in the heat and humidity. "Son, if you were going any slower, you'd be moving backward!" the coach said. "Take a hike!" The chubby kid trudged off the field, beaten.

"Maybe you're being a little sensitive," Nick told Morgan. "As you can see—it's not just you. Don't take it personally."

"Huh!" Morgan huffed. She walked away from him, headed for the dugout and a seat on the bench. "Let Nick think what he wants," she grumbled. "*I* know it isn't fair."

Practice was finally over. It was five o'clock as Morgan and all the boys headed back into the school building. "All right, gentlemen," the coach told them, "hit the showers!"

Morgan stood there, wondering what he expected *her* to do. Didn't she count? Wasn't she even here?

"Hudson," he called to her, motioning for her to come over to him. "I saw that diving catch you made today." He gave her an appreciative nod.

Morgan melted, flashing a big smile. Finally, a compliment! She'd been totally wrong about him!

"Really?" she asked, trying to sound casual.

"Yeah." His smile vanished. "If you were a little quicker, you wouldn'ta had to dive, and you woulda made the throw."

Morgan wilted. She could feel her whole body sag with disappointment.

Just then, Nick walked by, headed for

the boys' locker room. "Hold on there, Lighter," the coach hailed him.

Great, Morgan thought. Now he's going to tell Nick what a great job he did today. Just what my ego needs right now.

"Coach, I need to shower," Nick protested.

The coach's face grew somber. "Maybe you better take one at home. Cut!" he said, running a finger across his throat.

Nick's eyes looked like they were going to pop out of his head. *"What?"* he gasped.

Morgan, too, was flabbergasted. Yes, she'd played better than Nick today, but he'd been pretty good. . . . Just how good did you have to be to make this team, anyway?

Morgan followed Nick all the way home, begging him to see reason. "Nick, it's not my fault you got cut!" she told him as they entered the Lighters' den, where the magic jersey was kept, safely on its shelf.

Nick was in no mood to be reasonable. Angrily, he threw down his glove and backpack. "Oh, really?" he yelled. "I guess it's just a big coincidence. Out of all the positions you could've gone after, you chose mine!"

Out of the corner of her eye, Morgan thought she saw the jersey move, but she didn't pay much attention. My imagination is going haywire, she figured. It must be because she was upset—as she had every right to be. Nick was not only her cousin, he was one of her best friends in Fairfield.

"Nick," she said firmly, "you know I've always played shortstop. I played five years of Little League in that position."

"Was this before or after ballet lessons?" Nick asked sarcastically.

"Nick, grow up!" Morgan shouted, exploding. "If you think I'm only doing this so you can't play, you're crazy!"

Nick ignored her. "I don't know why you're doing this, but the bottom line is: There is no place for a girl on that team— not even a girl who acts like a guy!"

"What?" Morgan demanded. "That's not fair, I—"

"Oh, forget it, Morgan," Nick went on. "Maybe you *should* be on the team. Maybe you *are* a guy, after all."

Morgan felt like she'd just been hit with a right uppercut from Laila Ali, her favorite boxer. The room spun for a moment before coming back to normal. Morgan even thought she saw the magic jersey sliding into her backpack. She shook her head violently, to clear it. Had Nick really said that to her? Was it possible?

"That doesn't even make sense!" she protested, as Nick walked out of the room, ending the discussion.

Alone, Morgan reached for her backpack, figuring she might as well head home. "I don't act like a guy," she said out loud, to no one in particular.

"Or do I?" she wondered.

Could it really be true? Did she act like a guy? Could Nick possibly be right, for once in his life?

CHAPTER FIVE

IMAGE IS EVERYTHING

The next day, Elliott came to school as E-dog. He was dressed in a black-leather jacket and had just spent an hour in front of his bathroom mirror doing his hair in spikes. It had taken half a tube of hair gel to get it just right, but it was worth it. Dark shades completed the look.

For the first time in his life, Elliott looked dangerous.

Elliott checked himself out in the glass

of the school doors, and nodded approvingly. Awesome. He *was* E-dog!

No longer would jerks like Coach Bender be able to bust his chops. His new crew had his back, and even though they weren't too bright, they sure were intimidating.

Today, he would show Coach Bender, and the rest of the world, that the little guy could not be kept down forever. He would stand up to the man, fight the power, beat the system.

Actually, Elliott wasn't quite sure how his current plan would achieve all that— but he knew he had to do *something*—and he was about to pull a prank he'd always thought it would be cool to try. He'd just never had the nerve to do it . . . until now.

Just before lunch, he met Rory Bunkley and his buddies at the far end of the main hallway. There, they opened the door of the custodian's closet, and took out a plunger and several rolls of toilet paper.

Then they made a quick dash to the Boys' Room, where they grabbed two freshmen who were in the middle of washing up and shoved them out the door. Once they were alone, the guys opened up all the stall doors, and Elliott went to work.

"You sure you know what you're doing, E-dog?" Rory asked doubtfully.

E-dog was busy with the plunger, stuffing rolls of toilet paper tightly into each toilet bowl. "Watch and learn," he told Rory and the others, giving them a smug smile.

What these guys don't understand, he thought, is that water has to have someplace to go. If it can't get into the bowl, it will back up through the pipes, and out the other side—into the girls' bathroom!

E-dog put down his plunger and hit the flush lever. He hurried through each of the stalls, flushing each toilet in turn. The pipes gurgled and rumbled. "Let's go! We're out of here!" E-dog yelled and they all fled into the hallway—just as the first screams came from the Girls' Room.

"Surf's up!" Rory crowed.

E-dog was exhilarated as he strutted out into the hallway. His buddies all clapped him on the back, whooping and laughing, congratulating him. The crew started down the hall. E-dog couldn't believe he'd just gotten away with—

The door of the Girls' Room flew open, and three girls ran out, all soaked with yucky water, and covered with bits of soggy toilet paper. Elliott stopped in his tracks when he saw that one of them was Nick's older sister, Hilary. A chill ran down his spine. Oh, no! He was totally busted!

Hilary's beautiful wavy red hair was a total mess. She scanned the hall furiously, looking for the idiots who had done this to her. And her eyes fell on E-dog.

"Elliott!" she screamed, her eyes widening in shock and fury.

"S-sorry, Hil," Elliott said meekly. He'd been nailed—and by Hilary Lighter, of all people.

"Grrrr!" Hilary growled. She rolled up her soggy sleeves and lunged at Elliott.

E-dog rushed down the hall after his laughing buddies, his E-tail between his E-legs.

THE JERSEY

• • •

Morgan had taken about all she could. She'd spent a whole day feeling tortured over what Nick had said to her. Did people really think she wanted to be a boy? She'd never, ever thought of herself that way. . . . Sure, she was a good athlete and loved sports. But so what? Everyone had always told her she was pretty. . . .

Ugh. Thinking about it was driving her crazy. Morgan didn't know what to do. She figured she could ask 'Slaw and Elliott what they thought . . . but they hadn't wanted her to try out for the baseball team, either. Wouldn't they just agree with Nick? Morgan finally decided she needed the advice of another girl—one who was nothing like her, but who was older and possibly wiser. She called her cousin Hilary. After all, they did have one thing in common—they both had to deal with Nick on a daily basis.

Morgan told her cousin that she really wanted to talk to someone in person, so Hilary agreed to come over right away.

Now Morgan lay sprawled on her bed, waiting for her cousin to show up. She'd been reading an issue of her favorite sports magazine. There was a great article in it about Laila Ali, Muhammad Ali's daughter, one of the best female boxers around.

Morgan had been admiring Laila's picture on the cover—she sure was pretty, and that didn't stop *her* from being an athlete. If Laila could box, why couldn't Morgan play baseball?

Morgan heard the doorbell ring downstairs. Moments later, Hilary walked into Morgan's room and flopped down on the bed. Hilary's hair was all tangled, and there were bits of paper in it. "What's up, Hil?" Morgan asked.

"I don't want to talk about it," Hilary said flatly. "But since you asked, Elliott and his new buddies decided to pull a prank, and I got the bad end of it. When you called, it sounded like you wanted to talk right away, so I didn't have time to get cleaned up."

"Oh," Morgan said, concerned. "What did they do?"

"*Hello?* Didn't I say I don't want to talk about it?" Hilary paused, and flashed a little smile. "I got them back good, anyway."

Morgan grinned. "Really? How?"

"Simple," Hilary said in a superior tone. "I turned them in to the principal. But enough about me and my problems— let's talk about *you*."

• • •

E-dog sighed. The Detention Room was beginning to feel like a home away from home. He, Rory, and the "Line of Pain" filed in and took their usual seats. Coach Bender watched them, shaking his head in mock dismay. Obviously, he was enjoying the moment immensely.

"Oh, Bunkley, Bunkley, Bunkley," he said to Rory, leaning over him. "You didn't make the baseball team two years ago, you flunked out of shop . . . look at you! Your life went right into the toilet. Now, is that what you were looking for when you pulled this prank? The life you flushed away?"

Rory shifted uncomfortably. Elliott sat watching, weighing his options. What would E-dog do in this situation? He had an uncomfortable feeling that E-dog wouldn't let anyone pick on his friends. . . .

"This kind of nonsense," the coach went on, "doesn't take *brains*, Lugnut—"

E-dog cut the Coach off. "Achieving the perfect geyser," he said condescendingly, "is a precise science, requiring the proper ratio of paper to water—or resistance versus force."

Take that! Elliott thought. E-dog is tough *and* smart.

"Ohhh," Coach Bender said, smiling cruelly. "It's 'Mr. I-Can't-Keep-My-Mouth-Shut-While-Other-People-Are-Talking.'"

Elliott stuck his chin out defiantly. "You can call me 'E-dog,'" he said coolly.

"So—you have something to say about this waste of space?" Coach Bender asked, spreading his arms out to include the whole room and everyone else in it.

"Yeah!" Elliott said proudly. "*I* am the waste of space!"

No, wait, he thought. That's not what I meant to say.

"I mean," he corrected himself, "I did it—I'm responsible."

Elliott could feel every eye in the room on him. This was his moment—his finest hour. In his mind's eye, he could see the lights in the room dimming. Spotlights searched the room and found him. In the background, a heavenly choir was singing the Hallelujah Chorus. The crowd, adoring him, shouted over and over again, "E-dog! E-dog! E-dog! E-dog!"

The coach's voice snapped Elliott back to reality. "E-pooch, E-mutt—whatever your name is," he said in an acid tone. "Take a seat, pal. You're gonna be here awhile."

Elliott looked around at the bare room . . . and at the sorry figures of his pathetic new friends. What was he doing? Here he was, mouthing off to a teacher while he was in detention! "Yes, sir," he mumbled in embarrassment as he slowly lowered himself into the seat. "Thank you, sir."

"Nick is such a jerk!" Morgan said, finishing her tale of woe. "Who says I can't be on the baseball team?"

Hilary gave her a long look. Then she said the last thing Morgan wanted to hear. "A better question is, why would you *want* to be on that team? They yell . . . sweat . . . stink . . ." Hilary wrinkled her nose in disgust.

Morgan sat there in stunned silence. She'd called Hilary for support, for sympathy, for guidance. What a mistake. She should have remembered that Hilary hated sports with a passion.

"On the other hand," Hilary continued, "you've always been a tomboy. So I guess if you're into that kind of thing . . ."

"Tomboy?" The word cut Morgan like a knife. She hadn't been called that for a long time, but now the painful memories flooded back. It was what the kids had called her before she moved to St. Louis. The girls who didn't like sports had always made fun of her . . . and so had the boys, whenever she played better than they did. Oh, how she hated that word.

"You should be more interested in going to the mall and highlighting your hair," Hilary counseled. "Maybe Nick was right," she finished with a shrug. Then she laughed. "Boy, there's a first!"

Morgan didn't laugh. In fact, she felt like crying. "What's wrong with me?" she asked softly.

Realizing she'd hurt Morgan's feelings, Hilary stopped laughing and grew serious. Gently, she took Morgan's hand and held it. "There's nothing wrong with you," she assured her.

"Really?" Morgan asked doubtfully. "My favorite color's blue. . . ."

"Blue's a great color!" Hilary said emphatically. "Easy to accessorize!"

Morgan waved a correcting finger at her. "It's my favorite color because the Indianapolis Colts wear blue. Not many girls choose their favorite colors because of football teams." She heaved a great, heavy sigh. "I'm a disaster!" she moaned.

Hilary took Morgan's face in her hands. "Morgan, I can help you," she promised. "If you are willing to do whatever I say."

Morgan hesitated. Should she really

put her whole future into somebody else's hands? Especially someone totally different from her? On the other hand, what did she have to lose? She couldn't stand the idea that people were mocking her behind her back, calling her a tomboy. "Okay," she agreed reluctantly.

Hilary flashed her a beaming smile. "Great! Now the first thing you have to do is—quit baseball."

"No!" Morgan cried, pulling away from her. "I love baseball!"

"You *have* to quit," Hilary insisted. "You promised to do whatever I said, remember?"

Morgan sighed. "Okay," she said heavily.

"Good," Hilary said. Then she saw the magazine—the one with Laila Ali on the cover—lying on the bed. Hilary picked it up, holding it away from her like it was diseased. "And get rid of this," she ordered.

Morgan winced. Now she couldn't even read her favorite magazine? What had she gotten herself into?

"Morgan," Hilary said with a smile, "it's time to get in touch with your feminine side."

Morgan nodded, submitting to the inevitable. Hilary was right. She *had* to do this. She was a girl, and she wanted to be like other girls. Only, why did it mean she had to give up everything she loved?

Hilary got up and went to the door. "This is a major renovation," she said excitedly. "I have to go hit the Web." She rushed off, leaving Morgan alone in her misery.

"I didn't realize I was *that* bad,"

Morgan said glumly to the empty room. She got up off the bed and grabbed an empty cardboard box. "No more baseball," she said wistfully, tossing her mitt, her batting helmet, and several hardballs into the box. "No more hockey. . . ." In went her leg protectors. "No more volleyball . . . no more Rollerblading . . . no more football."

Her sports equipment now filled the large carton. Finally, she tossed in the magazine with the photo of Laila Ali. As she did so, she felt something wrapping around her right ankle.

Her heart skipped a beat. Looking down, Morgan saw that it was the magic jersey. It was halfway out of her backpack, and gripping her leg tightly.

In an instant, Morgan's body began to shimmer and disappear, as a blinding blue light filled the room. The next thing Morgan knew, she was tumbling through space.

Seconds later, she found herself in the middle of a boxing ring. She could feel boxing gloves on her hands, a plastic mouthguard in her mouth, and protective gear on her head. It was a good thing, too—because standing opposite her was none other than Laila Ali herself—and Laila's vicious right hook was coming straight at Morgan's face!

CHAPTER SIX

IN THE RING

Morgan ducked just in time—but she didn't see the quick left hook that followed. It landed flush on her jaw. After that, all Morgan saw were stars, as she fell to the floor in a heap.

The next thing she knew, she was staring up into Laila Ali's concerned face. "Hey, are you okay?" Laila asked her.

"I . . . think so." Morgan got up, trying to master her rubbery knees. "Laila Ali?"

She still couldn't believe she was here, in the ring, with one of her idols.

Laila helped her up. "Good," she said. "You know who I am. But do you know who *you* are?"

"Yeah, sure . . ." Morgan said uncertainly. "I'm . . ."

But who was she supposed to be, really? Morgan had no idea. "I'm, um, I'm fine!" she said cheerfully, ducking the question and buying some time to think.

"All right," Laila said. "Let's go. Another round." She started to move and shuffle, stepping lightly around the ring in a graceful but dangerous dance.

Morgan stood still, watching her in confusion. "You . . . you want me to *fight* you?"

"Yeah," Laila said cocking an eyebrow. "I'm not here to get a manicure. I've got a match coming up." She moved toward Morgan, who backed away.

Laila danced after her, shadowing Morgan's every step. "Going somewhere?" she asked.

"I . . . I . . . I'm just helping you with your footwork," Morgan improvised. She darted away from the boxer.

Laila stayed close on her heels. She sent out a punch that just barely grazed Morgan's shoulder.

"Aaaagh! Owww!" Morgan shouted, grateful the blow had missed its mark.

"'Ow?' Who says 'ow' when they're boxing?" Laila asked, clearly amused.

"People who get hit," Morgan answered under her breath.

Laila looked confused. "What?"

"Nothing."

Laila kept on coming. It was all

Morgan could do to duck, or to block the constant punches that came her way. Once or twice, she had to cover her face with her boxing gloves. Finally, she just ran right into Laila and pushed her away.

Quickly, Morgan made a sign with her gloves. "Time out!" she called. "Time out!"

"Hey, what are you doing?" Laila asked, frowning. "You're my best sparring partner—you know there are no time outs in boxing!"

So that's who I'm supposed to be! Morgan realized. She took a quick glance around the dimly lit gym. She saw punching bags, weight-lifting equipment, and jump ropes. Nearby, other boxers quietly practiced their punches. On the side of the ring, a photographer seemed to be setting up for a modeling shoot.

"Whoa! Look out!" Morgan told herself, ducking one last furious punch before the bell mercifully sounded. "Uh! The bell. Thank you!" she said. Saved by the bell, Morgan thought, literally.

Laila headed to her corner. Morgan followed her, curious to find out more about why she was here. Morgan figured the jersey had a reason for sending her into the boxing ring.

"Uh, your corner's over there," Laila told her. She gave Morgan a concerned glance. "Are you sure you're okay?"

"Oh . . . yeah," Morgan said, embarrassed. But she stayed where she was. "Can I ask you something, Laila?"

"Sure," Laila said, sitting back on her stool and toweling off.

"Why do you do this?"

Laila looked confused. "Do what?"

"*This*." Morgan gestured around the gym. "Fighting—sweating and getting hit and dirty—I mean, well, sometimes, don't you feel like . . . like you're not a girl?" She grimaced, hoping she hadn't offended Laila Ali by being so direct.

At that moment, two little boys who looked about nine years old came up to Laila's corner. One was holding a water bottle, the other a bucket. "Laila, ready for some water?" the first boy asked, his eyes wide with awe.

Laila took the water and had a swig of it. The second boy held out a bucket, and Laila spat the water out. Both kids looked up at her like she was their biggest hero.

"Thanks, guys," the boxer said, giving them a smile. "You'll be in my corner when I win the championship."

Exhilarated, the boys raised their fists

in triumph and marched off, chanting, "Ali! Ali! Ali! Ali!"

When they had gone, Laila turned back to Morgan, ready to answer her question. "I'm a lady *and* a boxer," she explained. "And I intend to be the best at both. Now, if you're 'girl' enough, let's go a couple more rounds."

Morgan felt a weight lift off her shoulders. Flashing Laila a grateful smile, she nodded. "I'm girl enough."

The bell rang, and Laila and Morgan headed for the center of the ring, putting their gloves up once again. Morgan concentrated as hard as she could. Sports demanded the best of a person, she knew—especially when you were up against someone who was way beyond your ability, like she was now.

How could I ever have thought of

giving up what I love the most? Morgan wondered, as the punches rained down on her protective headgear. What was I even thinking?

CHAPTER SEVEN

THE FINAL BLOW

"Life really stinks," Nick muttered. He and 'Slaw were in the Lighters' den, tossing a football lazily between them.

"I hear you," 'Slaw replied, sighing in agreement.

"There's no justice, I tell you," Nick said. "If there was, you and I wouldn't have been cut. You were definitely the best catcher out there."

"Maybe." Coleman shrugged. "Maybe not."

"Sure you were," Nick insisted. "And if it wasn't for Morgan, I'd still be up for shortstop."

'Slaw gave him a long look. "She's pretty good, Nick. Good as you."

Nick scowled back at him. "Girls," he said disgustedly. "They can be such a pain."

"Ahem!" Nick whirled around to see his sister Hilary standing there, wearing a hot-pink blouse, and looking even girlier than usual. "I'm glad you're here, Nick," she said, her hands on her hips. "I needed to tell you something." She paused for dramatic effect. "You're a jerk!"

Nick looked back at her dully. "You can't hurt me, Hilary," he told her. "Coach already cut me from the baseball team. Nothing matters anymore."

"Well, maybe you got cut because

you're a jerk?" she suggested.

Nick sighed. "Is this going somewhere, Hil?" he asked, trying to hurry her along.

"Okay," Hilary said, her annoyance bubbling to the surface. "You told Morgan that you think she acts like a boy—which is a mean thing to say. And who cares what you think, anyway? Except, now Morgan thinks—well, actually, Morgan doesn't know what to think. Except *I* think—"

"Ooo! Ooo! Lemme guess," 'Slaw broke in. "Nick's a jerk?"

"Very good," Hilary said, nodding as Nick elbowed Coleman hard.

"Well," she continued, "the good news is that Morgan's quitting baseball altogether. You accidentally did something right!" Giving him a little smile, she turned and flounced out of the room.

Suddenly, Nick didn't feel so good. He hadn't really meant what he'd said to Morgan. She was feminine enough—that had to be obvious to anybody. She'd just made him so mad that he'd wanted to hurt her back. But now that he knew he had, he felt sorry about it. And the worst part was, he couldn't take his hurtful words back, now that they were out of his stupid mouth.

He looked guiltily over at Coleman, who just stared at him, saying nothing.

Nick blew out a long breath and squared his shoulders. He knew what he had to do, and the sooner he did it, the better.

Elliott glanced at his watch. It was only 4:30. So why was Coach Bender erasing the words WELCOME TO DETENTION from the blackboard?

THE FINAL BLOW

The coach turned to the assembled detainees and announced: "I'm letting you delinquents out early today. Not that you need to know, but I happen to have a meeting with a big shot from the athletic department at the U. of M."

His chest puffed up as he said it, and he gave them a smug, superior smile. "I'm outta here! Yes!" he hissed.

Picking his jacket up off the desk, the coach left the room. The moment the door closed after him, Rory turned to Elliott with an evil grin. "Okay, Idea Guy," he said, waggling his eyebrows. "Where do we go from here?"

Elliott smiled back at him. "Home?" he suggested hopefully. He was getting tired of being E-dog. Detention was incredibly time-consuming, and he preferred his old buddies in the MNFC to this sorry bunch.

"Cool!" Rory said, nodding. "Hey, guys—party at Rifkin's!"

"No, no, no, n-n-n-n-n-no," Elliott corrected him hurriedly. "There's *never* a party at Rifkin's."

In an instant, the whole gang turned on him. Their smiles vanished, and they leaned menacingly toward him.

Elliott looked around desperately. He knew he had to think of something, or he was going to be shark food. His eyes fell on the fire extinguisher hanging on the wall near the door. An idea popped into his mind. He chuckled to himself, amused at the thought of it . . .

Rory growled into his ear. "You think it's funny to uninvite your friends—squid?"

So now he was "squid" again? After all he'd done for them? Elliott would have resented it—if he hadn't been totally scared out of his shoes right at the moment.

"No, absolutely not!" he assured Rory, doing his best to look innocent. "I was just thinking . . ."

Here it came. Elliott sure hoped they liked the idea—if they didn't, he'd never get out of this room in one piece. "I was thinking—Bender's meeting this guy from U. of M. What if when he opened his office door, there was . . . oh, I don't know . . . a surprise?"

They followed his gaze to the fire extinguisher. Sneers spread slowly across their faces as they realized what Elliott was getting at.

Elliott grinned, too. He was home free. And after all, it was just a suggestion. He had no intention of going through with it. Elliott had had enough of detention and enough of these bad dudes.

But the thought of ruining the Coach's job interview *did* make him smile. . . .

Moments later, Elliott stood at the door of Bender's office flanked by Rory and his gang. Rory shoved the fire extinguisher into Elliott's chest, hard. "Fire when ready," he ordered.

Elliott was trapped. Surrounded. What was he going to do?

He pushed the extinguisher back to Rory. "I really don't think we should be doing this," he said.

"You thought of it," Rory pointed out.

"Yes," said Elliott. "A 'thought.' That doesn't mean it has to be followed up by action. See, that's the difference between humans"—here, he pointed to his own chest—"and the rest of the animal kingdom." He pointed behind him, to where the "Line of Pain" lurked.

Rory didn't get it—or if he did, he didn't like it. Roughly, he shoved the extinguisher back at Elliott. "What's up, E-dog? Are you chicken?"

Elliott shoved it back again. "Actually, I believe my original classification was 'squid.' Either way, I'm outta here." He turned toward the exit.

The group converged around him, blocking his way. "Not so fast, pal," Rory said, thrusting the fire extinguisher back into Elliott's hands. "You're the brains behind this operation."

"Somebody needs to be," Elliott muttered. Defeated, he took the fire extinguisher, and pointed it toward the open office door. There was no going back now. He was doomed.

Closing his eyes, Elliott pulled the trigger.

CHAPTER EIGHT

AN ATHLETE AND A WOMAN

Morgan was beginning to get the hang of this sparring stuff. She was even beginning to enjoy throwing a punch or two at her opponent, in between dodging Laila's wicked shots.

There was a left jab, followed by a right cross. For a split second, Morgan saw an opening and launched a right of her own, nailing Laila on the side of the head.

"Hey! Good one!" Laila encouraged her. "There you go!"

AN ATHLETE AND A WOMAN

The bell sounded. Morgan smiled, pleased with herself. Once again, she followed Laila back to her corner.

"Way to tough it out," Laila told her.

"I guess I was just having a bad day," Morgan said with a shrug.

When Laila's trainer began unlacing her gloves for her, Morgan understood that the sparring session was over. She knew that soon, the jersey would flash her back home. But she wasn't ready to leave—not yet. Not until all her questions were answered.

"Laila," she said, "do you really have to work hard to be in a man's sport?"

Laila's gloves were off now. She removed her headgear and gave Morgan a sharp look. "It's not a *man's* sport if *I'm* in it." There was warmth in her voice, but there was steel, too.

Morgan nodded thoughtfully. "I never thought of it that way . . ."

Laila took a towel from her manager and dried the sweat off her brow. Morgan noticed that she was wearing really cool earrings. She'd had them on the whole time.

"Didn't people tell you that you couldn't do it?" Morgan asked. "Didn't they say it was just for guys? That it wasn't 'feminine'?"

"Sure they did," Laila answered. She smiled, adjusting one of her earrings. "They told me I was crazy for trying. But my strength as a woman adds to my strength as a fighter—if I do say so myself." She winked at Morgan, and fluffed out her long, shiny black hair.

"Didn't it hurt your feelings when they said all that?" Morgan wanted to know.

"It used to," Laila acknowledged. "But I know I'm doing this from the bottom of my heart. I do it for the same reasons you do."

Morgan blinked. "Which is . . . ?"

"Because I love it," Laila said simply. "And you've got to do what you love, no matter how hard it is."

"No matter how hard it is . . ." Morgan repeated. She knew she'd never forget Laila's advice.

Laila stepped down out of the ring. Pulling some lip gloss out of her bag, she turned back to Morgan and smiled. "Gotta look pretty for the camera," she explained, heading over to where the photographer was waiting. He began to snap pictures of her in fighting poses. Laila flipped her hair, looking totally glamorous, yet tough at the same time.

Morgan admired her so much. That was exactly the way she wanted to be. Grabbing a towel, she pushed through the ropes to leave the ring. As she stepped through, her legs got tangled in the ropes. The jersey caught on one of the clips that held the ropes, and it pulled her back. . . .

There was a blue flash. Morgan's body shimmered like a desert mirage, and vanished into thin air. The original sparring partner returned to her own body and completed Morgan's fall in the ropes, landing clumsily on the gym floor.

Laila looked at her. "I'm glad you box better than you walk," she said wryly.

"Morgan?" Nick entered Morgan's room tentatively. He wasn't sure she'd welcome him, considering the way he'd treated her.

She didn't seem to be there, yet her

mom had said she was upstairs in her room. So where was she?

He spotted the copy of ESPN magazine at the top of Morgan's carton of athletic gear. Nick picked it up and started leafing through it. Laila Ali was pretty cool, he had to admit.

Suddenly, Morgan landed right on top of him! Nick tumbled to the floor, while Morgan rolled backward onto the bed. "Whoa!" she cried.

Nick got up, steaming. She didn't have to attack him just because he'd said one mean thing to her, did she?

But Morgan didn't look angry at all. In fact, she was beaming. Then Nick saw the jersey, and he instantly understood. "Where were you?" he asked, getting to his feet. "A wrestling match?" He rubbed his side where it was sore from hitting the floor.

"Close. Boxing!" Morgan said excitedly. She handed the jersey back to him. "Nick," she said, "you know y—"

"I'm an idiot?" Nick finished for her.

Morgan looked at him, clearly surprised. She'd probably expected him to argue with her. "Right!" she said.

"Now before you start yelling at me," he began, "Hilary said you were quitting the baseball team."

His words came out in a rush. He'd thought long and hard about what he wanted to say, and he wasn't going to give her a chance to interrupt until he'd finished. "You shouldn't quit, Morgan. You've got the glove and you've got the talent . . . and if you're the first girl to make the Fairfield High baseball team, then that'll be awesome. Don't quit," he repeated softly, taking her by both shoulders and looking into her eyes. "You're too good."

Morgan gave him a thousand-watt smile. Nick smiled back. The two cousins high-fived each other, then hugged affectionately. They were friends again—and when Nick and Morgan were on the same team, they were unbeatable.

CHAPTER NINE

YOU'VE GOT TO HAVE FRIENDS

Their work done, E-dog, Rory, and the others walked slowly, casually down the hallway. They could see Coach Bender coming toward them, talking with a man in a blue suit and red tie. Coach was wearing his jacket and tie, too, Elliott noticed. He could tell by the way the coach was acting that he really wanted to make a good impression on the man from U. of M.

Elliott could hear Coach all the way

down the hall. "So as you can see," he was saying, his arm on the other man's shoulder, "I've stepped up the program a few notches. And it's all based on three key elements—focus, committment, and—"

He paused, spotting Elliott, Rory, and the others as they passed him by. "And . . . respect," the coach finished, swiveling around to frown after the boys.

E-dog led his crew coolly down the hallway a few more steps. Then they slowed down, looking back at the coach, waiting eagerly for him to open his office door.

The coach continued to eye them warily as he led the other man slowly toward his office. "Because, if you don't have the respect of the players," he went on, "you don't have the respect of the community. . . ."

The coach's hand was on the doorknob,

Elliott noticed, licking his lips. True, he'd tried to back out of this one, and he was sure he was going to be sorry afterward. But there had been no way out—and it was too late now. He figured he might as well enjoy this moment to the hilt. He stood at the corner of the hallway, watching intently. Rory and the others huddled behind him.

"And without the respect of the community," the coach continued slowly, his eyes still on the boys, "what do you have, really?" He yanked open the office door— and a tidal wave of suds cascaded down onto him. Coach's feet went out from under him, and his arms flailed wildly as he fell backward into the hallway, carried by the foamy wave.

It sent him sliding past the man from the U. of M., who stood there, stunned.

E-dog and his friends got a good, long look at the coach's richly deserved come-uppance. Then they all took off down the hall like a shot—all but Elliott, who couldn't resist one last glance at the hapless coach.

Coach Bender got up slowly, slipping a couple of times along the way. His face was so covered with white foam that he looked like a white-bearded Santa Claus. But his expression was decidedly un-jolly—and it turned even uglier when he saw Elliott.

"Rifkin!" he growled, murder in his eyes. His hands came up like a couple of claws, and he leaped toward Elliott.

Luckily for Elliott, the floor was covered with suds, and the coach took another tumble before he'd even gone a step. *Un*luckily for Elliott, the minute he turned around to flee, he was grabbed harshly by the collar. He looked up meekly into the stern face of Miss Pinchly, the meanest teacher in the whole school!

"I didn't do it!" Elliott cried, but Miss Pinchly just scowled at him, obviously not buying his story.

Rats! he thought. Busted again!

"Man," he muttered, "I am so *bad* at being bad!"

Elliott got out of detention by explaining that he'd been forced into playing the prank on Coach Bender. Rory and the others had surrounded him, he claimed. And with his reputation as an A+ student, he was allowed to escape detention—on probation. That meant that if he ever got into trouble again, he'd serve both the new detention and this one. That was fine with him. E-dog was gone, and Elliott Rifkin steered clear of trouble.

The next morning, when he got to school, Elliott's heart was in his throat. He knew that Coach Bender would be looking for him.

Even worse, Rory and the boys would not exactly be pleased with him for pinning the fire extinguisher prank on them. In fact, he'd be lucky to get through the day in one piece. Elliott knew he needed protection. He also knew where to get it— from his real friends, the Monday Night Football Club.

Nick and 'Slaw were at their lockers. Elliott made a beeline for them. He was almost there, when he heard Rory's voice calling him.

"Well, if it isn't the *squid*!"

So we're back to squid, Elliott thought. He edged closer to Nick and 'Slaw, and turned his back as Rory and his buddies strutted past.

Nothing happened. Rory and the "Line of Pain" didn't hit him. They didn't shove him. They didn't even say another word to him. He was nobody to them again, just as he used to be. Boy, did that ever feel good.

"What happened to your new look?" Coleman asked him, noticing that Elliott wasn't wearing his leather jacket or shades, and that his hair was back to normal.

Elliott ran a hand through it. "All that hair gel was eating up my allowance," he joked. Nick and 'Slaw laughed, and they all high-fived each other. It's good to be back, Elliott thought. Better than good— it's great!

• • •

Morgan was at the other end of the hall, near the gym, checking the list to see whether her name had been cut. Several names, including Nick's and Coleman's, had thick red lines drawn through them. But her name was still there.

Suddenly, she felt a finger tapping her on the shoulder. She turned around, and found herself staring into the scowling face of Coach Bender.

"Hudson," he greeted her.

"Coach?"

"I heard you were quitting."

Morgan shook her head. "You heard wrong," she told him emphatically.

The coach nodded slowly, eyeing her approvingly. "Well, you got hustle," he said, patting her on the arm. "And drive."

Morgan felt a thrill of pride go through her. She was about to open her mouth and say thank you, but Coach stopped her.

"But—" he added, chuckling, "you don't have an arm. So, you work on that, and there might be a spot for you—next year."

Morgan felt all the wind go out of her, as if she'd been punched by the likes of Laila Ali. "Next year?" she repeated.

The coach smiled sincerely, and indicated the list. "Cut," he said. Taking a red pencil out of his pocket, he crossed off her name. Then, turning to her, he gave her an apologetic shrug. "Keep trying, Hudson—you got what it takes. Don't give up."

"I won't," Morgan promised, disappointed but determined. Her pride intact, she walked down the hall to where the other members of the MNFC stood in front of their lockers.

"I got cut," she told them matter-of-factly, then heaved a weary sigh.

"I feel your pain," Elliott said sarcastically. Obviously, having been cut before he ever got started, he didn't have too much sympathy for her.

"Welcome to the team," 'Slaw said, giving her a friendly pat on the arm.

Nick stepped forward. "I'm getting that shortstop position next year," he informed her, cocking an eyebrow.

Morgan smiled, and took up the challenge. "Yeah? You can back me up," she told him. "Ride the bench for a season."

Coleman and Nick stepped back as if they'd been burned by her fiery wit. "Uh-oh. Uh-oh," they said together.

THE JERSEY

They all laughed—four best friends enjoying the moment. Finally, all the members of the MNFC were back on the same team.

The following afternoon, the Monday Night Football Club got together to hang out. It wasn't Monday night, of course. But it had been a long, long time since the four of them had spent an evening of watching sports. Baseball tryouts had come between them, pitting them against each other in fierce competition. And then there had been Elliott's little adventure as E-dog, flirting with reform school.

In the Lighters' den, where the magic jersey was back on its shelf, the Saturday afternoon baseball game was on TV. The Tigers were beating up on the Blue Jays, 10–4, and it was only the third inning.

Not much excitement there.

'Slaw and Nick sat on the couch, munching on potato chips and idly tossing a Koosh ball between them. Elliott stood in back of the sofa, with "punch-me" pads on his hands, while Morgan practiced her boxing moves.

"Laila Ali is so awesome," she raved, bobbing and weaving the way Laila had done. "She floats like a butterfly, and she stings like a bee . . ." Suddenly, Morgan had a great idea. "Hey—that could be her motto!"

Elliott gave her a look. "It's been taken," he said flatly, arching an eyebrow.

"Oh. Right. Of course. I thought it sounded familiar," Morgan said with a little grin. Bouncing up and down, she threw a few soft punches at Elliott's outstretched hands.

"I don't like fighting," Elliott

complained, drawing the pads away protectively.

"Boxing, Elliott," Morgan corrected him. "It's totally different. It takes finesse . . . control . . ." She hauled off and threw a roundhouse right at him, to make her point.

Elliott saw it coming, and ducked just in time. Morgan's fist carried through the spot where he'd been, and continued around, her body spinning with it—until she hit Nick right in the kisser!

Nick dropped like a rock. "Oh, Nick!" Morgan gasped. He must have gotten up off the sofa while she had her back turned! Now he lay on the floor, dazed.

At that very moment, Hilary came into the room. Seeing Nick on the floor, and Morgan standing over him, her fists in boxing position, she frowned deeply. "See, this is exactly the kind of behavior we were talking about, Morgan," she scolded.

Morgan gave her a meek little smile and shrugged. "Um . . . sorry?" she said.

She was sorry—sorry she'd decked Nick. But she wasn't sorry that she was who she was. Like Laila Ali, she was an athlete and a woman. And she always would be, no matter what anybody said.

FROM THE JERSEY #8
NEED FOR SPEED

CHAPTER ONE

LEADER OF THE PACK

"Let's go, Rifkin, let's go!" Elliott Rifkin urged himself on as he huffed and puffed down Fairfield High School's red dirt track. There were no other runners in sight, and Elliott figured he had outdistanced the competition by a mile. It was warmer than normal for an early spring day and his blue T-shirt was soaked with sweat, but he didn't care. He was pumped and energized—today he felt as if he were invincible. He lengthened his stride, pretending he was long-limbed and tall, like his track-and-field idol, world champion Michael Johnson.

As Elliott neared the finish line, he was lost in dreams of the victory that lay just a few yards ahead. Suddenly, Elliott felt it didn't matter that he was a stocky freshman who was a good foot shorter than most of the other sprinters. It didn't matter because Elliott had the *heart* of a runner. Even if those other dudes had booster rockets on their shoes, they couldn't come within ten miles of Elliott "Breaking the Sound Barrier" Rifkin.

Lungs burning, Elliott burst across the finish line. Gasping for breath, he trotted a few steps, then came to a stop, doubling over with his hands on his knees. Runners were passing him now, but who cared? Elliott Rifkin had shown the world what he could do.

His buds from the Monday Night Football Club, Nick Lighter, Coleman "'Slaw" Galloway, and Morgan Hudson jogged up from the sidelines. "Fantastic, Elliott!" Nick cheered.

"Your personal best!" Coleman added.

"Way to go!" Morgan thumped Elliott on the back. She turned to her cousin Nick and waggled her eyebrows. "I knew our boy could do it!"

"Was that a win or what?!" Elliott gloated, straightening up. "I bet you're glad you hung around to watch the try-outs after all! You didn't think I could do it, did you?" Elliott grinned broadly.

Nick, Morgan, and Coleman were Elliott's three best friends. All four fresh-men were sports freaks, which is why they had formed the MNFC. Nick had not only founded the club but he had inherited a magic football jersey from his grandfather. Elliott had been sure Nick was teasing him when he talked about putting on the ratty old yellow-and-blue jersey and being transported into the body of a professional sports star. But Elliott had seen the magic happen with his own eyes. Nick had been transported into the body of NFL star Steve Young right in the middle of a 49ers game. Morgan had found herself in the body of Kurt Warner—the St. Louis Rams quarterback. Elliott, who adored sports statistics, had taken on the job of keeping a detailed record of the jersey's adventures and how it seemed to work. At first the jersey had seemed to work its magic only when Nick and Morgan were wearing it. Then 'Slaw and Elliott discovered if they put on the jersey and touched one of the two cousins, they too could experience the thrill of becoming their favorite athlete.

Morgan gulped. 'Slaw winced. Nick cleared his throat. Before any of Elliott's pals could speak, the track coach ambled up.

Elliott gasped, still trying to catch his breath. "Coach, how'd I do? I kinda left everybody in the dust there, huh? That's all right, though. Some of those guys look like they have real potential." He pushed back the damp strands of red-brown hair plastered to his forehead and grinned up at the coach.

Nick, Coleman, and Morgan shared a worried glance. "Uh, Elliott . . ." Nick began.

The coach stared down at Elliott and shook his head in disbelief. "Hate to break the news, Rifkin, but those guys with potential lapped you big time."

What? Elliott's jaw dropped as he realized that he had finished an entire lap behind everyone else. He wondered briefly whether that meant he still had to run the final lap, but one glance at the coach told Elliott that he shouldn't bother. Still shaking his head, the coach glanced at his clipboard. Elliott cringed as the man drew a big black mark through his name. "Sorry, buddy, you're cut. You might want to try out for the chess team."

"The chess team?" Elliott swallowed hard.

"Do we even have a chess team?" Nick muttered.

Morgan shot her cousin a dirty look,

then slung an arm around Elliott's shoulder. "It's okay, man."

"Yeah," Coleman added as the four friends headed off the field toward the lockers. "Don't worry about it. It's gonna work out fine."

Easy for you to say, Elliott thought glumly. Straight-A Coleman hasn't got a clue what it feels like to come in last for anything. Elliott sighed, feeling sorry for himself. On top of everything, thought Elliott, I don't even know how to play chess!

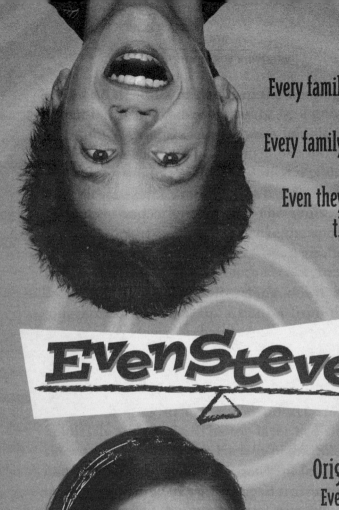

Every family has a Louis.

Every family wants a Ren.

Even they can't believe
they're related.

EvenStevens

An
Original Series
Every Weekend
on

Disney
CHANNEL ℠

ZoogDisney.com